Raindrops

Written by Sandy Gay

Pictures by Dorothy Stott

SCHOLASTIC INC.

New York   Toronto   London   Auckland   Sydney

Copyright © 1994 by Scholastic Inc.
All rights reserved. Published by Scholastic Inc.
Printed in the U.S.A.
ISBN 0-590-27370-1

9 10   08   00 99 98 97 96

Drip, drip, drop.

Rain is falling on my house.
Drip, drip, drop.

4

Rain is falling on my window.
Drip, drip, drop.

Rain is falling on my hat.
Drip, drip, drop.

Rain is falling on my flowers.
Drip, drip, drop.

Rain is falling on my dog.
Drip, drip, drop.

Rain is falling on my dad.
Drip, drip, drop.

Rain is falling on my house.
Drip, drip, drop.